KINK IN THE ROAD
THE MEN OF TRINITY BAY

EVIE MITCHELL

THUNDER THIGHS PUBLISHING PTY LTD

Cover design and illustrations by Laras Putri
Editing by Emerald Edits and Aquila Editing

ACKNOWLEDGEMENT OF COUNTRY

I acknowledge the Traditional Custodians of the lands on which I write, the Ngunnawal people, and pay my respect to elders both past and present.

I acknowledge the continued and deep spiritual relationship of all Australian Aboriginal and Torres Strait Islander peoples' to this land, and their unique cultural and spiritual relationships to the land, waters and seas and their rich contribution to society.

CONNECT WITH EVIE MITCHELL

Facebook
Greedy Readers Book Club
TikTok
Instagram
Bookbub
Goodreads
Newsletter

BLURB

On a small island town where single women are rarer than a unicorn sighting, I've always been the odd woman out. As the town's go-to grease monkey, I'm more "bro" than "babe", which is great for finding friends and not-so-useful in my search for love.

In an effort to draw women to our small town, our matchmaker mayor decides to play Cupid with a singles weekend—only I'm left playing wallflower rather than bell of the ball.

That is until Aiden and Finn, the smokin' hot pub owners I've been crushing on, admit they don't see me as the town's perpetual little sister....

"Kink in the Road" is a steamy, romantic romp that'll have you believing in the power of love, laughter, and a well-oiled...machine. After all, the best things in life come in threes!

CHAPTER 1

"We have a woman problem."

The words were so startling—especially coming from our pioneering, feminist mayor—that I dropped my ratchet.

"Indeed, we do," my father agreed.

I jerked, clonking my head on the underside of the car I'd been repairing. Grunting back a curse, I rubbed the rising welt as I strained to hear their conversation.

"The census results don't lie," the mayor continued. "There are fifty men for every woman on this island. And while I'm sure there are a portion who aren't interested in marriage, or the opposite sex, or having a family for that matter, there will be a portion who are."

I glanced around the tire of the vehicle I was currently under to see my dad nodding. Dressed in an old and dirt-stained boiler suit not dissimilar to my own, he leaned against the office door, sharing a cup of coffee with our mayor.

Agatha Dorante, in contrast, looked ready to walk into the boardroom of a Fortune 500 company. While they both had a shock of silver hair, Mayor Dorante's lay in a tightly contained bob, while Dad's flew about in wispy tufts.

The mayor—dressed in a burgundy silk button-up dress that she'd paired with black heels and pearls—seemed immune to the chaos—and mess—of our workshop.

Our apprentice bustled in and out while our office manager handed over keys and issued invoices.

"If I know anything, Agatha, I know you have a plan."

She nodded. "Singles weekends."

I thumped the ratchet against the car's undercarriage for effect, but all my attention had become hyper-focused on their conversation.

"You think that'll work?" Dad asked, his tone skeptical.

"I've already had over fifty women sign up."

He whistled low. "Well shoot, that's promising."

"I'm going to need help to wrangle the visitors over the weekend. Can I count on you?"

Dad ran a hand through his hair, leaving a trail of grease and muck. "This is our busy season, you know. What with spring approaching and all."

The small village of Trinity Bay sat at the northern tip of Kink, the northernmost island of the Isle of Astipia. With a population of less than five thousand people, the island had attracted few migrants over the years due to its wicked winters and tightly held land. It was, however, a popular tourist destination for foodies looking to try farm-to-table fare, or our local seafood delicacies.

Many of our young people inherited their businesses—either the farms or the boats—though some worked to capture the energy generated by our powerful waterfalls and strong ocean currents for the hydroelectric company, using that energy to pump power to the mainland.

Others worked for the island's second biggest employer, the distillery, making whiskey, gin, and vodka of all kinds. We were famous for our alcohol and rugged beauty—drawing tourists by the thousands each year.

But few stayed. And even fewer of those who did stay were single women.

Agatha pushed Dad again. "Please, Bruce. If not you, then surely Riley could be spared."

I started.

"Ry? Well now, that's a thought."

I could practically see the ancient cogs turning in my father's mind.

No, no, no, no, no—

"Riley could do with some women friends." He shook his head in a gesture that had become all too familiar. "Poor love. All these men and not a one who sees her as anything but a sister."

Done with eavesdropping on conversations I knew better than to listen to, I turned back to my work, determined to get this stubborn engine finished before dinner time.

Alas, despite my efforts, their voices carried across the cool concrete floor toward me.

"We're hosting a series of four events over the weekend—with a free day on the Sunday for further mingling. Friday we begin with a welcome brunch at the pub, followed by a treasure hunt and then a singles mingling event in the evening. On Saturday, we'll host an extended lunch on the green, followed by a series of outdoor activities such as a walking tour, boat ride and so forth. Saturday evening is a cookout. Sunday will be a sit-down brunch then free time." The mayor rubbed her hands together. "It's going to work, Bruce. I can feel it."

I tried and failed not to roll my eyes as I

began to scrub at decades of ancient grease and thick, rich mud from the axel of old Bob's car.

Really, Bob. A car wash wouldn't have killed you.

"And you want Ry for what?" Dad asked.

"We need service staff. I know Riley has helped at the pub a few times over the years."

A fat clump of muck cracked away, hitting me in the face.

Thanks, Bob.

Considering I'd been under this car for the last three hours, I didn't want to know how much gunk might be covering my body.

"I suppose I can spare her for one weekend. Ry," he called. "Take tomorrow off. You're going to help with the singles weekend."

I gritted my teeth at his assumption that I didn't have anything better to do with my time.

Why does everyone assume I wouldn't be interested in attending as a participant? Am I not a woman? Am I not worthy of love?

"Okay," I responded, frustrated and hurt but unwilling to allow them to hear that in my voice.

The mayor left and Dad returned to work on a tractor that we needed to get finish.

I ignored his cheerful whistle and took out my frustration on the stubborn vehicle.

I'd read a news article recently about small towns in America where women were outnumbered by men. The article had talked about how women felt unsafe. That wasn't how I felt in this town. Not even close. Our men had been raised to respect women.

It'd started when I was five and my mother passed away. Dad had tried his best, but he'd been a wreck, barely able to function after her loss.

Without asking, the town had stepped in, rallying around one of their own in our time of need.

Food had appeared in our fridge and freezer. Friends would "stop by for a cup of tea" only to clean our house and sort our laundry. I'd been whisked away to sleepovers and playdates with the boys who'd taught me to dig up worms and where the best spots were for finding lizards and frogs.

Slowly Dad and I had come out of our grief, but the town's determination to take care of us had lingered far into my early adulthood.

When I'd graduated high school, I'd decided to leave the island for a few years to attend college. That gap had opened my eyes to the world—and the delights of men who didn't view me as a little sister.

But my heart and soul would always be in this land. There wouldn't be another place for me —this was where I was born, and it would be where I remained until my last breath.

When the first machines had reached the shores of our island, my many-greats-grandparents had seen their chance to leave the cold and dangerous waters of the fishing industry behind. Through grit and determination, they'd forged their own path, establishing our mechanic shop and building our legacy.

A legacy I feared might die with me if I couldn't convince at least one man to look at me with something besides friendship.

Giving up on Bob's wreck, I slid from under the car. "Dad, I'm calling it a night. You need me to stick around?"

He popped his head out from behind his office door and I could see he was already washed and ready to head home.

"No, love. You want to join me for a meal?"

I shook my head. "I'll get something from the pub."

"I'll see you Monday. Say hi to those boys for me."

I nodded, knowing without asking who he meant. Tourist season wouldn't begin for another few weeks, which meant that the locals had the pub to ourselves—at least for the moment.

I cleaned the workshop, clearing the grime and grease that always defined a day's work. Each night the workshop went from chaos to calm coordination, each tool meticulously checked and returned to its place. It had become my habit to do so, a habit that had been ingrained in me from the cradle.

Take care of your tools, and your tools will take care of you, my grandfather had always said. And while that remained true, a clean shop also helped customers gain a sense of confidence in our expertise and service.

I finished cleaning and moved into the staff-only bathroom at the rear of our big workshop. We'd upgraded our premises a few years back, building a bigger and better garage so we could service more of the giant farm machines that the locals had begun to use. Along with that change had come heated concrete floors, better ventilation, and a new staff area including a bathroom with a shower.

In a town this size, one would assume we wouldn't have much work. But between the hydroelectrical plant, the tourists, and the agricultural customers, we made a tidy profit.

I caught sight of myself in the mirror of the bathroom and sighed. Dirt and grime peppered my face, highlighting my blue-green eyes. My blonde hair had slipped out of my ponytail and formed knots and dreads caked with dirt. Grease smeared my overalls, and I had a thick layer of dirt under my nails.

"And I wonder why no one wants to date me."

I might have a pretty face under all the grime, but one could hardly look past the dirt, my height, and my stature. I was no dainty fae, but a mountainous maid built for lean winters and bountiful summers. My wide shoulders, large breasts, and generous hips were a testament to the generations of strong women who had birthed my line.

Those traits might have helped my family in the past, but they did nothing to advance our

DNA now. Alas, the men of this town did not seem to find me attractive.

"Their loss."

Grumbling quietly, I cleaned up as best I could then locked the shop and walked the short road down into the village proper.

Early blooms of lavender, lilac and jasmine guided my path down the cobblestoned road and into our village center, their perfume light and sweet. The colors of the blooms reflected in the setting sky—a horizon of oranges, purples and pinks. I paused at the top of the hill, admiring the evening sky.

The cool breeze from the ocean brushed across my face, teasing my hair while salt touched my lips.

My frustration—an emotion I had acknowledged but refused to unpack—eased, leaving behind a bittersweet ache.

I wanted. I ached with want. A want for a partner to share sunsets like these. A want to fulfill dreams of travel and laughter, of shared memories and thoughts.

A want to love and be loved in return.

I kicked a pebble on the sidewalk, blowing out a long breath as I passed the trim cottages and sprawling gardens that lined our main street.

"Off home, are we?" Mr. Murdock asked, breaking my melancholy thoughts.

I forced a smile, stopping to lean against his garden fence, and admire his freshly trimmed roses. "Yes."

"Bert? Where are you—oh! Hello there, Riley!"

I lifted my hand in greeting to Mrs. Murdock, who stood at the door with her other husband, Roger. The Murdocks were a typical family for our small town. Throuples had abounded for centuries as the women persisted. The government had even ruled polygamous marriages legal for anyone who married and lived on our small island, such was the recognition of our situation.

And yet I can't land a date.

"It'll be dark soon. Best be getting home." Bert clipped a small rose from his bush, gently removing the thorns before handing it to me. "Go with kindness, darling."

I accepted the flower and returned the greeting, tucking the bud in my hair as I set off for the pub.

I lived in a small cottage at the back of the pub. I'd moved in with Dad upon returning to the island, but my childhood home had become too much for us to manage, and I had needed my own space. After agonizing over the decision, we'd decided neither of us needed a house with eight rooms—or the electricity bill that came with heating it.

A newcomer and his partner had moved to the island with the intent of opening a bed and breakfast. While our island may be small, real estate was at a premium and there had been a lovely profit for Dad upon the close of sale. He'd purchased a small cottage close to town, placed most of it in his retirement fund then handed me the rest.

It now sat in a bank account accruing while I considered what to do with it.

My first thought had been to buy a house, but I'd quickly dismissed that idea, content to rent until the right place came along.

The two-bedroom cottage had originally been a small stable for the pub. The previous owner of the pub had converted it into a storage shed, and the current owners had converted that into a tidy little rental.

I adored my small home, appreciating the care that had been taken to lovely restore the original stonework and preserve the wooden beams. The cottage had a small courtyard with a high stone wall that removed it from view of the pub, giving me the appearance of privacy.

I pushed through my small gate and walked under the overgrown wisteria and ivy that grew over the arbor beside my house, to the back door in the stone wall that opened to the rear of the pub parking lot. A scant eight steps later, and I was pushing open the heavy wooden door of the ancient pub.

Built before most of the village had even been a thought, the pub had gone through many generations of hands before the most recent publican had passed away, willing the entire thing to a distant cousin.

And it was that distant cousin—and his friend—that had me visiting far too many a night.

I tucked my hands in the pockets of my overalls and headed to the bar. Like a beacon, my senses immediately identified where the two men were. Aiden manned the bar, his smile flashing as he joked with locals. Meanwhile, Finn stood at the pass, controlling the kitchen with his brisk efficiency.

I slid onto my usual bar stool and waited for Aiden to make his way down to me, taking the time to observe the men.

Aiden with his dark hair and green flashing eyes would have made a charming pirate—sailing the seven seas and seducing each and every lass or lad who caught his eye.

Unlike Aiden, whose tattoos painted beautiful stories across his skin, Finn had no visible tattoos or body piercings—though tiny scars marked his arms and across his hands, marks from a career spent with knives and hot metal. Finn kept his sandy-brown hair cropped close to his head, and I knew from experience that his stunning blue eyes could flash with fire. Both stood either at my height or a fraction taller.

Aiden had inherited the pub, and its raft of issues and financial pitfalls. Enter Finn. They'd pooled their money, investing their time and effort into the pub, clawing it back slowly from the brink of financial ruin to build it into something special.

Aiden interrupted my musing by placing a glass of non-alcoholic cider in front of me.

"Hard day?" he asked, in his usual charming way.

"Long day," I responded, forcing myself to shove away my shimmering flit of attraction. "You?"

He shrugged. "We're busy preparing for the singles weekend." He flicked a lock of dark hair out of his eyes then placed his forearms on the bar, leaning toward me as his green eyes danced with mischief. "You attending that?"

I grimaced. "Apparently."

His eyebrows rose. "Really?"

My gaze darted to Finn, who stood at the pass watching us as his hands automatically assembled plates of steak with thick cut fries and fresh grilled vegetables.

"The mayor roped me in." I sighed, glancing down at my hands. "Seems I'm to help you and Finn out here."

"You're unhappy with hanging out with our lovely selves?"

His question reignited frustrated needy ache in my chest.

"No, it's fine, it's—" I forced myself to stop speaking, biting the inside of my cheek to keep the words from spilling out.

"It's?" he prompted, his green gaze searching mine.

"Nothing." I turned away, lifting my beer. "Gonna go play some pool."

He placed a hand on my arm, halting me as I tried to slide from the stool. "Are you okay?"

For some strange reason, the care in his voice broke through my hardened exterior, hitting the vulnerable woman underneath.

No, I wanted to say. I'm lonely.

Tears burned the back of my eyes, and a lump clogged my throat.

I want, I burn, I need.

I forced a laugh, pulling my hand from his. "I'm fine." I nodded at the bar. "And you have patrons waiting."

I stepped away, ignoring the way his gaze seemed to burn into my back.

Taking a long drag of my drink, I glanced over at the pass to see Finn staring at me, his gaze narrowed.

Forcing a reassuring smile, I turned away from him and moved to the pool tables.

Those boys aren't for the likes of you.

CHAPTER 2

"You have nice eyes," the out-of-towner informed me as we battled for supremacy across the pool table. "They're like the blue of a sapphire."

"Thanks," I muttered, lining up my shot.

The hour had grown late, and the pub crowd had slowly thinned out until it was just me, Finn and Aiden, and a handful of tourists left. I knew I should have left earlier, but the thought of going home filled me with despair. I couldn't say why I felt that way, just that this strange malaise had descended. A yawning, empty, hollow feeling had settled in my chest, and the idea of being alone with it felt almost dangerous.

The tourist, whose name I'd forgotten, shifted to behind me, leaning over my body. I stiffened, pressing myself into the table as he moved closer.

"Need a hand?" he asked, his breath hot against my ear.

"No." I took the shot then stood, stepping away from him as unease slithered down my spine. "Your turn."

He took an age to decide how he would play the shot, brushing past me multiple times before finally leaning over the table to attempt to sink the ball into the hole.

He failed.

Any enjoyment I might have had quickly evaporated as he became bolder, and sexually aggressive, his flirting taking on an almost possessive edge.

"Look," I said as he crowded me into the table once more. "I'm not interested, okay?"

I might have been lonely, but I wasn't desperate.

"Bullshit," he smirked, reaching for my hip. "You've been flirting with me for the last hour."

"No, I haven't. I've been—"

He stepped into me, his hand snaking up to grab the back of my head as his lips descended toward mine.

I struggled to twist away, pain shooting through my scalp where his hand fisted my hair. His lips glanced the corner of my mouth as I managed to turn my head. His alcohol-laden breath filled my nostrils as he slurred a chuckle.

"Playing hard to get, little girl."

"Let me go," I demanded, shoving at his chest. "I don't want—"

I fell forward as the guy abruptly released me. Stumbling, I nearly tripped only to have strong arms wrap around me, pulling me into a hard, warm chest.

I jerked up, twisting to find Aiden had me, but he wasn't watching me—his hard gaze was trained on Finn and the tourist.

"The lady," Finn barked, shaking the tourist by the cuff of his shirt, "said no."

The man swung wildly, attempting to break Finn's hold. Long used to drunken antics, Finn easily dodged the guy, tripping him up and forcing him to stumble toward the door. He glanced at me over his shoulder. "You want to press charges?"

I shook my head. "Just get him out of here."

Finn did so, easily maneuvering the man until he could toss him outside. He pulled the heavy wood closed and turned the lock. It was only then that I clocked that I was the sole remaining patron of the pub.

"Where'd everyone go?" I asked, my mind racing as I tried to process the last few minutes.

"Home. It's nearly midnight."

I closed my eyes and leaned into Aiden. This moment wouldn't last—soon I'd be cold and alone once more.

A warm hand touched my face, and I blinked my eyes open to find Finn staring at me.

"You okay?" he asked, his gaze searching.

I nodded. "Thank you."

His jaw clenched, his blue eyes flashing with frozen fire. "Don't fucking thank me. I should have punched the fucker in the face."

I could feel the anger radiating off him. It burned ice cold, barely controlled behind his normally calm façade.

In an uncharacteristic move—and one that I would blame on shock—I stepped out of Aiden's arms to wrap my own around Finn.

"Still," I whispered against his chest. "Thank you."

Finn remained stiff for a beat before his arms wrapped around me, squeezing me tight. "We should have intervened earlier."

I memorized his smell—the mix of sweat and heat that clung to him. He'd removed his apron and chef whites, leaving him in a surprisingly clean black shirt.

I stepped back, an embarrassed flush heating my cheeks. "I should go." I forced a rusty laugh. "Though who knows if I'll be able to sleep after this. My adrenaline has certainly spiked."

I felt them both stiffen.

"Or," Aiden said slowly, exchanging a look with Finn. "You could stay."

I raised an eyebrow in question.

"We could play a game." He nodded at the table. "Just until your nerves settle."

I glanced at Finn, who nodded, then back at Aiden. "You guys aren't too tired?"

His slow smile unfurled a delicious warmth in my belly.

"Never for you."

CHAPTER 3

The game felt like the antithesis of my previous match. The men were jovial and teasing, but maintained a respectful distance.

Too bad when all I wanted was to be disrespected by them in the bedroom.

Such was my life.

I sunk the ball in the far pocket and pulled back from the table, grinning in satisfaction. "Seems I won."

"So it seems," Aiden agreed, handing off the cue to Finn. "But we all know I'm a terrible shot."

'Twas true. Aiden had to be one of the worst players I'd ever witnessed. For a man normally possessing of grace, he reminded me of a baby giraffe when a shot became available—all lanky limbs and uncoordinated movements. Adorable.

I waited for Finn to rack the balls, absently grinding chalk into the tip of my cue.

"Why did you look like you were going to cry earlier?"

Finn's unexpected question snapped me out of my mini-daze.

"When?" I asked, frowning as he finished lining the triangle with the balls.

"When you first walked in." He glanced up as he shuffled the balls to place the black eight in the center. "Did something happen at work?"

A weird lump formed in the center of my chest while a strange, not unpleasant, sensation squirmed in my middle.

"You were in the kitchen, how could you tell I was upset?"

Finished with the balls, he removed the triangle and hung it on the hook, blowing my mind with his offhanded comment as he did so.

"I always know," he said, his back to me. "Every day you're the light that sits at the end of our bar. And tonight..." He turned, his serious gaze finding mine. "You were shrouded in darkness."

I glanced at Aiden, stunned by this revelation.

He lifted his beer bottle and tipped it at Finn.

"He speaks truth." He inclined his head to one side. "A problem shared is a problem halved."

God, how I wanted to share my feelings with them, to unburden this need that writhed and wriggled, clawed and called inside me.

But how did anyone explain this ache in their chest? This unrepentant and unreciprocated longing?

I swallowed rapidly and glanced away, biting my tongue to halt the avalanche of words that threatened to burst from my lips.

I want to be looked at as a woman. I want to be kissed and caressed. I want to come home to laughter rather than silence.

I knew how to live alone—I'd been doing so for years. And I knew I could continue to do so happily. This loneliness would pass, it always did.

I glanced at the two men and forced a strained laugh. "It's nothing, promise."

Finn frowned, his dark eyes flashing. "Liar."

I coughed. "Excuse me?"

"Liar," he repeated, folding his arms as he glared at me. "For months there's been something off. I thought it was the workload or the season, but tonight is the first time you've come into our bar looking like someone kicked your dog."

"I don't have a dog," I murmured, stunned that he'd noticed.

"What he's saying," Aiden said, jerking a

thumb at his friend, "is we're worried about you."

He laid a hand on my arm. "We're friends, right?"

I stared down at the hand on my skin. His fingers were long and blunt, thick with the slight rasp of a callous or two on his palm.

"Friends," I murmured, lifting my head to stare at Finn. "I... I think so."

"Good." He nodded once, as if that resolved it. "Then unburden yourself."

My tongue loosened, my heart-need finding voice before I registered what I was saying.

"I'm single, but not invited to the singles weekend. No one in this town—or on this island— sees me as a woman. They don't look at me and think, 'oh, there she is. My future partner.' They look at me and see a mechanic, a little sister, a friend. I'm never anyone's choice. And I want to be."

I thrust the pool cue at Aiden and whirled away, running agitated hands through my hair. "I want to be someone to someone. I want to be a partner and a wife. I want adventures and laughter and fights and all the little intimacies that come with being with someone."

The words hurt to say, and the raw longing in my voice hurt to hear.

"I ache with it," I admitted, tearing myself open. "I'm lonely—so fucking lonely—but that doesn't mean I want to settle." I glanced over my shoulder, seeing their stunned expressions.

What have I done?

My nose stung with repressed tears, my chest tightening as heat flushed my cheeks. Humiliated, frustrated, embarrassed, I swallowing hard—desperate to leave before I did anything stupid. "I have to go."

Finn hand wrapped lightly around my wrist, staying my dramatic exit

"Thank you for sharing." He stroked his knuckles across my cheek. "You deserve everything your heart desires."

You, my heart whispered. *I want both of you.*

I glanced away, shame burning my cheeks. "I need to get to bed. It's late and we have the singles weekend to support tomorrow."

Finn hesitated before he dropped his hand and stepped back. "Let us walk you out."

"It's only twenty-eight steps home," I protested.

"We're walking you home," Aiden confirmed, slinging an arm over my shoulder to give me a hard squeeze. "No arguments."

With Finn on one side of me and Aiden on the other, we crunched across the gravel lot toward the small door in the stone wall.

Squished between them like this, I couldn't help but imagine this were a different universe—one in which we were a throuple, walking home from a long night.

Why do I do this to myself? That possibility is so foreign, so out of reach I might as well be living on Mars.

We made it to my door and I pushed it open into the darkened house.

"Well, this is me." I fought for a lightness I didn't feel. "Thanks for… everything."

Finn and Aiden exchanged a look before Aiden stepped forward to pull me into a tight hug. "Good night, *oeh'uru pahlke*," he whispered, brushing a kiss against my cheek.

I stiffened as he pulled away, surprised by the term of endearment he'd whispered in the island's native tongue.

Our pulse.

Before I could think on it further, Finn crowded in, backing me up until I was inside my small cottage.

He caught me in his arms, one behind my back, the other burrowed in my hair.

Stunned, I blinked up at him, confused beyond belief.

"Don't doubt yourself," he said roughly. "You're a beautiful woman, Riley. Desirable and lovely both inside and out."

I spluttered—too shocked by this moment to do anything but stare into his dark, gorgeous eyes.

He leaned down, brushing a kiss against the opposite cheek to Aiden.

"Sleep well, *pahci oeh'uru sahoehuke*."

Piece of our soul.

He let me go and knocked a knuckle against my door. "Lock up tonight." He pulled it closed behind him, leaving me to stand—aching and stunned—in the entry of the cottage.

I raised my hands to cup my cheeks, the feel of their lips burning against my skin.

"What the hell just happened?" I whispered into the dark.

The dark—unsurprisingly—didn't answer.

CHAPTER 4

Our town had never seen so many single women. In a rainbow of colorful dresses, skirts and blouses, they had descended upon our fair shores, chattering and giggling, bright-eyed and hopeful as the men of my town attempted to sweep them off their feet.

The sun shone brightly on the town green as I helped Aiden and Finn to set up for the picnic brunch. They'd spent the morning preparing an array of succulent sandwiches, crisp salads, and decadent desserts, and now we were arranging everything on long tables draped with cheerful gingham cloths.

"Pass me that fruit platter, would you, Riley?" Aiden called from the far end of the table.

I hefted the heavy tray and made my way over to him, trying not to dwell on the memory of last night.

The guys acted normal this morning, as if

they hadn't blown my mind with their declarations and gentle cheek kisses.

I wasn't sure if I was relieved or disappointed.

As I handed Aiden the platter, our fingers brushed, sending a jolt of electricity through me. His green eyes met mine, a hint of a smile playing at the corners of his mouth.

"Thanks, oeh'uru pahlke," he murmured, just loud enough for me to hear.

I guess we weren't pretending nothing had happened after all.

Before I could find the words to respond, Mayor Dorante bustled over, clipboard in hand and a determined gleam in her eye.

"Everything looks wonderful," she said with a brisk nod, her silver bob shimmering with her movement. "But I need a favor from you three."

Finn joined us, wiping his hands on a hand towel. "What can we do for you, Mayor?"

She consulted her clipboard. "We're short a few people for the treasure hunt. Would you mind joining in? We need one more group of three to even out the numbers."

I opened my mouth to decline, thoroughly uninterested in being the additional wheel on a singles weekend—but Aiden beat me to it.

"We'd be happy to help," he said smoothly. "Right?"

To my surprise, Finn nodded. "This is all set up. Just needs to be unwrapped."

"Excellent." Mayor Dorante scribbled

something on her clipboard. "You'll be teaming up with Colleen and Warrick."

Against my better judgement, I followed her over to the couple, nodding my greeting to Warrick.

I'd known Warrick since birth. He'd grown up a street over from me, and at just nine months older than myself, we'd spent many a day rambling through the countryside getting into all sorts of mischief.

A few years ago, he'd set up a tour company to guide people around the island, along with his business partner, Del Bellinger. They lived up in the mountains in a small cabin that backed onto the national park. While Warrick was social, Del rarely made it down the mountain, preferring to spend his time away from people.

I eyed him, hiding a smile. The normally wild-looking Warrick had managed to subdue his riot of auburn curls and groom his beard into some semblance of respectability. He'd traded his trademark scuffed jeans for a pair of fresh dark-washed jeans which he'd paired with a new black shirt.

He stood an inch or so shorter than my own nearly six-feet, but what he lacked in height, he made up for in breadth. His muscles earned through hard labor and thousands of hours of chopping wood.

"This is Colleen," the mayor introduced. "She's from the mainland. Colleen, meet Aiden,

Finn, and Riley. They run our local pub and auto shop."

We all exchanged greetings, and I couldn't help but notice the way Colleen blushed at all the attention. Short, plump with a lovely head of tawny hair, she reminded me of Melissa McCarthy—gorgeous and cheerful, though a little shy.

"How are you liking our island?" Aiden asked Colleen, drawing her out of her shell.

"It's beautiful," she said, adjusting her grip on her cane. "I think I'm in love already."

Warrick grinned, his teeth flashing against his beard. "Wait till you see the mountains. You'll never want to leave."

She glanced down at her walking cane. "Are there accessible trails?"

"Aye," Warrick said with a nod. "But if not, I'll carry you."

Her cheeks flushed pink once more as I hid a grin.

"No Del today?" I asked him.

Warrick shook his head. "He's finishing up a tour. Though you can never know if he'll come to town or not."

The mayor called attention, using a microphone and a small portable speaker.

"Welcome to Kink Island," she said, inclining her head as the crowd applauded politely. "We're excited to have you here as we host our first singles weekend."

The applause included a touch more enthusiasm this time.

"I'd like to acknowledge our major sponsor for the weekend, *Speedy Singles,* for supporting the events."

She held up a small sheet of paper. "Our first official event is a treasure hunt. You'll receive a series of clues that will lead you to different places across the island. You'll need to collect the hints, find items, and get back here by midday. Our event will start when the bell tolls." She pointed at the clocktower in the distance which read twenty-to-ten. "And don't try to follow someone else—each team has a different randomized course." She gestured at the loaded table of good. "Now please, eat and mingle while you wait. You can collect your instructions and your first clue when the bell tolls. Good luck, everyone!"

We served ourselves as Colleen introduced herself.

"I live in Chars most of the year," she explained, taking a seat at one of the picnic tables on the green. Seated, she fluffed her skirt out, leaning her cane against the bench.

Warrick handed her a loaded plate, taking the seat beside her as Aiden, Finn and I took a seat on a picnic blanket spread across the warm grass.

"What do you do for a living?" Aiden asked, spearing a piece of pasta with his bamboo fork.

"I'm a supply chain manager." Colleen chuckled at our blank looks. "Basically, I get paid a lot of money to work from home managing temperamental vendors, suppliers and developers. I handle projects for companies all over the country, working to ensure that they have what they need when they need it."

I whistled low. "Sounds impressive."

She snorted prettily. "It's not."

I tilted my head to one side. "What brings you to this weekend?"

I saw her gaze dart toward Warrick before she answered.

"My friend signed me up. Said it would be a good opportunity to meet new people who want the same thing I do."

"And that is?" Warrick asked gently.

"A family. A home. Friends and community."

"Not love?" Aiden asked, raising one eyebrow.

Colleen shrugged. "Love would be nice, but mutual respect and attraction would be fine as well. Love can always grow."

"You'd be willing to move to the island?" Finn asked, reaching for my empty plate. "It's quite a way from most of the major cities."

Colleen shrugged. "As long as there's internet, I can work from anywhere."

"Lucky," I said, climbing to my feet and brushing off my butt.

The bells began to chime in the distance, heralding the start of the competition.

"I'll get it!" Aiden sprang to his feet, sprinting across the green to take one of the sheets.

Finn chuckled, shaking his head. "Be warned, Aiden's ruthlessly competitive. He might seem laid back but he's not a good loser."

We slowly made our way over to Aiden, who'd already ripped open the envelope and was poring over the contents.

"It's a riddle," he said, handing the clue to Warrick. "We'll have to decipher it to work out our first destination."

"'I have a head and a foot that are both the same size. Where I go depends on good fortune.' What do you think?" Colleen asked, peering over Warrick's shoulder.

"A coin," Finn and I said in unison. We grinned at each other, and I felt a flutter in my stomach.

"Right." Aiden rubbed his hands together, glancing between us. "We're off to the bank. Let's go."

"Wait," I interrupted, halting him with one hand. "The fortune is a clue. I think it's the wishing well."

Aiden slapped a palm to his head. "Of course it is."

We set off across the grass and I found myself walking between Aiden and Finn, their shoulders and hands casually brushing mine as we walked.

Around us, groups flowed, laughing and chatting—the women in their finery, the men appearing shiny. I glanced down at my worn and faded jeans and white, flowing blouse with a wry smile. I'd dressed for function and comfort, with just a hint of professional noting that I was meant to be working for Aiden and Finn—not attracting a potential mate.

"So, Riley," Colleen said, glancing back at me. "How long have you lived on the island?"

"All my life," I replied. "Except for a few years away at college."

"It must be nice to have such deep roots. I've moved around so much, I sometimes feel like I don't belong anywhere."

Before I could respond, Finn spoke up.

"Riley belongs here," the warmth in his voice was echoed by his slow, lazy smile. "Kink wouldn't be the same without her."

Our gazes met and I felt my cheeks heat. "I don't know about that."

Aiden bumped his shoulder against mine. "He's right, you know. You're the heart of this place. It's hard to imagine this town without you."

I ducked my head, unsure of what to say in response.

For so long I'd wanted what I couldn't have, hiding behind a mask of friendship that I struggled to free myself from the shackles of pining and flirt back.

We reached the wishing well, and sure enough, there was an envelope taped to the side with our team number on it. Aiden reached it first and eagerly tore it open.

"'What has keys but no locks, space but no

room, and you can enter but not go in?'" he read aloud.

"Fucked if I know," Warrick said with a shrug. "Any guesses?"

Colleen danced from foot to foot. "It's a keyboard, right? It has to be—space, enter, keys."

"Brilliant," Warrick beamed at her as if she'd performed brain surgery or flown to the moon. "It could be the library—there's computer there."

"Or," I said, fighting to hide a grin at Warrick's besotted look. "What about the organ at the church?"

"Yessss!" Aiden hissed, snapping his fingers. "Let's fucking go!"

Laughing, we followed him, matching our pace to Colleen's slower steps. As we made our way to the church, we pointed out different landmarks and places to Colleen, sharing stories and local legends.

"That's an *oech'snk* rock," I said, nodding toward the stone that sat in the middle of the library's front garden.

"A what?"

I grinned at her confused expression. "A fairy rock. Though we call them the little people. Sprites and spirits live inside it. If you've a need for help, leave an offering on the rock."

"That's darling." Colleen stopped, digging through her pockets to pull out a coin. "Let me make an offering."

While Aiden danced from foot to foot

impatiently, Colleen walked across to place a coin on the worn rock.

"Don't want to add your own?" Finn asked, his breath warm against my ear.

I turned, smiling. "I don't have a coin."

He reached up, brushing his finger against my ear. With a flick of his wrist, a coin appeared between his fingers. "Now you do."

Amused, I took the coin and walked across to the rock, standing next to Colleen as I placed it on the sun-warmed stone.

Silently, I bowed my head, asking for the one thing I wanted above all else.

Oech'snk, please guide me to my heart.

My palm tingled against the stone, and I swore I heard the whisper of a giggle as I raised my head.

Goosebumps raised the hairs on my arms as I stepped back.

"Are there other customs here that aren't on the mainland?" Colleen asked as we rejoined the group.

"A few," I said, trying to shake off my strange feeling. "You already know about the polygamous marriages."

"Yes, it's fascinating. But I suppose it was necessary."

"Very," Warrick agreed, falling into step beside her. "Women are revered here—they are the creators, the guides, the home. Our society is a matriarchal one, our women are the keepers of the hearth."

She tipped her head to one side, a little frown marring her brow. "I'm not sure I understand."

"The hearth was how we survived the winters," I explained, picking my way down the sidewalk. "Winters here are beautiful and brutal, filled with ice and snow and darkness. The heath is light and heat and survival. It is a symbol of hope that after the darkest day, the sun will return."

"So the women stayed home to tend the hearth and men did what?"

We all chuckled.

"No," I said, shaking my head. "Women on our island were warriors, hunters, gamekeepers. They owned boats and kept their own land. Our women are fierce."

Aiden bumped my hip. "Like you."

I grinned. "You should have met my mother. She was kind but ferocious. I miss her."

Finn caught my hand, intertwining our fingers to give me a squeeze. "She'd be proud of you."

On my other side, wrapped an arm around my shoulders, hugging me into him. "Very proud."

We left behind the rock and walked down the long street toward the church. A stone and wood building, it was one of the oldest buildings in the town.

Once upon a time, the ivy-covered building had been the township's bunk house, providing shelter for the first inhabitants. Over the centuries it had been many things—a hall, an emergency shelter, a storage barn. It was only in the early 1800s that the church had purchased the land and it had become a place of religion.

Father Donovan lived in the cottage at the rear of the church. He'd presided over nearly every birth, death and marriage for the last nearly forty years. Well into his sixties now, the spritely man regularly, and cheerfully ministered to his way-ward flock.

Aiden shoved open the ornate, heavy wooden doors, stepping into the quiet church.

Making our way down the long aisle, we began to search the organ pit, looking for an envelope.

The organ was one of the oldest and largest in all of Astipia. The town regularly had historians and musicians travelling through to view and play the gorgeous instrument.

No one was quite sure what had prompted the first Reverend Father to build something so unnecessary on Kink, but here it sat and here it would remain.

"I'll take this side," Aiden said, dropping to his knees. "Spread out. We need to find the clue."

Finn bent beside me, his shoulder brushing my own as we sorted through music books and under dusty sheets of paper.

"Can you work tonight?"

I glanced over at Finn. "Of course. If you need me."

His gaze met mine, his lips tilted up in a slight grin. "We always need you, Riley."

I swallowed against the lump in my throat. "You can't keep saying things like that. Not if you don't want me to get the wrong idea."

He brushed his knuckles against my cheek. "I think you're just starting to get the right one."

"Found it!" Aiden triumphantly held an envelope aloft.

This clue led us on a merry chase around the town, from the lighthouse to the library and down to the docks. With each solved puzzle, Aiden's competitiveness grew, and I found myself laughing more than I had in months at his enthusiastic aggression.

"'I have cities, but no houses. I have mountains, but no trees. I have water, but no fish. What am I?'" Colleen read out our final clue.

We all looked at each other, stumped.

"A phone?" Aiden asked, scratching his head.

"Which one?" Warrick asked.

Aiden shrugged. "Good point."

"What about a playground?" I asked, trying to solve it.

"what's the cities?"

I shrugged. "No clue."

Colleen giggled. "It has to be something obvious. Maybe we could work backwards? Where's somewhere on the island we haven't visited?"

"There's the police station," I said, frowning. "But I doubt they['ll want us there."

"Shit." Finn snapped his fingers. "I've got it . It's a map."

"Oh, fuck yes. Which means it's the old survey map in Town Hall." Aiden practically vibrated with enthusiasm. "That has to be it."

We hurried down toward the hall, dodging other teams as they darted to and fro, searching for their next clues. As we burst through the heavy wooden doors, we saw another team already there, searching the walls.

"There!" I pointed to the framed map hanging in a corner. The old parchment was worn and aged, yellowed by time and exposure.

Aiden lifted me without hesitation so I could reach the envelope taped to the top of the frame.

I ripped it open, quickly scanning the contents.

"The mayor's in her office. First team with all the clues wins."

Giggling like kids, we rushed down the hall toward the mayor's office and skidded inside. She sat at her desk, working on some papers.

"Ah, my first group." She grinned, leaning back in her seat. "Did you find all the clues?"

We handed her the envelopes, and she sorted through them, tallying our score.

"Well done." She reached under her desk and pulled a small cup-shaped trophy from the floor. "Here's your prize."

Colleen lifted the small trophy, plucking the slip of paper from its base.

"Two free drinks each at the pub." She glanced up. "Isn't that your establishment?"

Aiden's face fell. "It is."

The mayor snorted delicately. "You weren't meant to win."

"How about you take the trophy," I said, taking it from Colleen and handing it to Aiden. "And Colleen and Warrick can have the vouchers."

Aiden perked back up. "Works for me."

"And on that note, we should be getting back." Finn glanced meaningfully at his watch. "We've still got prep to finish before tonight." He flashed me a glance. "You're still helping, right?"

I nodded.

They left but Aiden ducked back in to press a kiss to my cheek.

"See you tonight," he murmured with a grin before leaving once more.

I pressed a hand to my cheek, staring at the door to the office.

"Well," the mayor said, sounding smug. "I see the weekend is already off to an excellent start."

CHAPTER 5

I worked beside Aiden, swirling cocktails, pouring wine, and pulling icy beer straight from the keg as the mixer got underway.

Mayor Dorante oversaw the entire event with a self-satisfied smile. She wove between clusters of couples and groups, welcoming the potential women to our fair shore.

"Seems like a lot of ado about nothing." Finn muttered, standing beside me as he sipped his water. Delicious platters heaped with canapés had streamed from the kitchen for the last two hours, their mouthwatering scent tempting my belly, which in turn rumbled reminders that I had yet to eat dinner.

"You think finding love is easy?" I asked, flipping glasses around to stack them in a rack for cleaning.

"Is this love? Or lust?" He waved a hand at the crowd.

"We have to start somewhere." I lifted the heavy rack and leaned down to slide it into the dishwasher. "Don't you want to find your person?"

I stabbed the start button then froze as an unexpected thought crossed my mind. "Wait, I mean—unless you, have?" I slid a glance at Aiden.

Finn's unexpected chuckle rumbled out of his chest, beckoning sly glances from the women on the other side of the busy bar.

"What's so funny?" Aiden asked, setting down a stack of dirty glasses.

"Nothing, I just—" I started, only to be, thankfully, interrupted by the mayor herself.

"And now for our next activity, speed dating. Please take a seat."

The participants settled onto tables, laughing and chatting as they sat across from a potential match.

With our jobs done for the moment, we stood at the back of bar, leaning against the bench top as we observed the proceedings.

Finn slid a plate of food in front of Aiden and I.

"Eat," he ordered.

Gratefully, I picked up a stacked sandwich, biting into it to find tender pieces of chicken flavored with a spicy satay and fresh, crisp vegetables.

Moaning in pleasure, I pulled a stool from

under the counter, taking a seat to watch the proceedings.

"Let's begin with some easy questions," the mayor called from the small stage at the front of the pub. "What is your favorite color?"

"Black," Aiden answered.

"Green," I said around a mouthful of sandwich.

"Pink."

Aiden and I both turned to stare at Finn. He shrugged.

"No judgment," Aiden said with a grin. "Any particular shade?"

Finn shrugged. "I'll let you know when I next see it."

"Favorite animal," the mayor called.

"Llama," I said with a tongue-in-cheek grin.

"Dog," Finn answered.

"Raptor."

I snorted, touching Aiden with the toe of my shoe. "How about choosing a living animal?"

"Who says they're not?" he answered with a grin. "I've seen Jurassic Park. You can't tell me those aren't real."

I snorted, turning back to watch the mayor.

"Alright, now we have the fun ones over, let's get serious." The mayor flicked through her note card. "What is your favorite sexual position."

The air seemed to get sucked from the room.

"Come on," she cajoled. "Most of you wouldn't be here if not for sex."

The tension eased at her joke as participants began to discuss their preferences.

"Partner on top," Aiden said after a beat. "I like to watch their expressions."

I dipped my head, concentrating like hell on the remainder of my sandwich as I tried—and failed—to stop myself from imagining Aiden in the bedroom.

"That works," Finn agreed, shifting beside me as he leaned against the bar. "Particularly if they're sitting on my face."

My blood warmed, heat simmering into a hot boil.

I'm about to spontaneously combust if they don't stop.

"But," Finn continued, sliding a thumb back and forth under his chin, "you know I like to be in charge."

"That's true," Aiden agreed as my heart sank. "Sex with you is like fucking a director. You're basically telling us what you want to see."

My entire being went up in flames of embarrassment and desire.

They're together. Damn it, I should have known this.

"How about you?" Aiden asked, nudging me. "Care to share?"

I swallowed around the lump of envy that sat like a stone in my throat. "Um, I'm not sure I have one."

I chanced a peek up from my study of the

crust to see they were both staring at me with raised eyebrows.

I dipped my head back down. "That is," I tried to clarify, "I tend to like any position so long as my partner is getting off on it."

"Ah," Aiden hummed as if he'd just found the meaning to life. "You're a sub." He gestured at Finn. "You two would be perfect together. He's a pleasure dom."

Curiosity got the better of me. "What's a pleasure dom?"

Finn plucked my uneaten crust from my hands and tossed it in the nearby trash. "I focus on my partners and giving them pleasure. I like to push my partners to their limits of pleasure before finding my own."

I swallowed, no longer fighting the images that played across my mind. "That sounds... restrained."

His slow grin reminded me of a wolf. "That's one way of putting it."

"And you?" I asked Aiden, curious at their dynamic.

He shrugged. "Switch. Top, bottom, sub, dom, up, down, round or straight—I just enjoy sex."

I glanced between them. "So you two are together."

They exchanged a glance.

"You could say that," Aiden said with a laugh.

"Yes," Finn confirmed, giving Aiden a stern look. "But we're also open to others coming into our relationship."

I mustered up all my courage, wanting to ask the question that burned on the tip of my tongue.

"Wha—"

The mayor interrupted me. "Where are the areas on your body you enjoy being touched?"

"Ears," Aiden said easily. "Someone nibbles on my earlobes and I'm a goner."

Finn tapped his lower lip thoughtfully. "The space between my shoulder blades."

"Feet," I admitted. "I melt whenever someone rubs my arches."

The men exchanged a look over my head.

"You know." Aiden leaned closer. "You have two feet."

I snorted. "I'm aware."

"And there's two of us...."

My face—already flushed—must have morphed into its own sun with the rate at which I blushed.

"I can count," I said dryly, braving my way through this minefield of a conversation.

"Just checking." Aiden winked at me then pushed off the bar to go serve a thirsty single searching for a drink.

"Shouldn't you be getting back to the kitchen?" I asked Finn.

He shook his head. "We're done for the evening. There's some dessert plates to lay out but one of the staff will take care of that. I'm off the clock until close."

"Oh." I fiddled with a loose thread on the knee of my jeans.

Finn's head dipped, his lips ghosting across my ear, his warm breath causing goosebumps to rise across my skin. "Ask your question."

I jerked, staring at him "W-what?"

Finn chuckled, his blue eyes dancing with amusement. "Ask, Riley. I know you want to."

Courage.

"When you said you were open to others in your relationship," I forced myself to ask. "What did you mean?"

"We're committed to each other, but we both know something is missing."

"Why do you say that?"

Finn brushed his knuckles against my cheek. "Because we met you."

CHAPTER 6

ecause we met you.

Finn watched me without judgment—he had laid his cards on the table and seemed comfortable to leave it up to me to decide where they fell.

"I—" I bit off a response, unable to process his statement.

He grinned. "Looks like the games are over. Let me help Aiden while you think about what I said."

He leaned in and brushed a kiss to my forehead. I closed my eyes, savoring the feel of his lips against my skin.

"No pressure, Riley. Everything is in your hands."

He left me sitting at the bar as the cocktail mixer broke up. Groups of people moved around the room, some leaving with their friends, some leaving as a couple or more. A few came to the bar but those were few and easily handled by Aiden and Finn, leaving me to sit and stew in my thoughts.

I wanted a family and home. I wanted a body —or bodies—pressed against me on cold nights. I wanted laughter and experiences, a life filled with joy.

If Finn were to be believed, I could have everything I'd ever wanted and more.

And I wanted, God, how I wanted.

I slid from the bar, needing some fresh air. Outside, I leaned against the old stone building, watching from the shadows as men I'd grown up with—attractive, charismatic men who treated me with respect but indifference—made fools of themselves in an attempt to attract a potential life partner.

But I didn't know where Aiden sat with this proposal.

"So ask him," I muttered, kicking a stone with my shoe. "Don't be a coward, Riley."

"Riley?"

I glanced up, surprised to see Del Bellinger standing in the shadows of the pub. The borderline recluse mountain man lived and worked with Warrick and made a decent living guiding determined hikers and climbers around some of the island's most treacherous and challenging trails.

Tall, broad, with a shock of dark brown hair and an unruly beard, he often reminded me of Bigfoot or a yeti, rather than the cute, shy boy I'd grown up with.

"Del, hey. How are you?" I jerked a finger back toward the door. "Did you go to the mixer?"

He stepped out of the shadows and into the light, pulling the knit cap from his shaggy hair. "Mixer?"

I chuckled. "Sorry, I forgot. Warrick said you were finishing with a tour group. "

"Aye," he murmured, watching wide-eyed as women streamed from the door of the pub, tumbling out in a colorful parade as they laughingly headed down toward the hotel. "I came for a drink but it appears I'm not the only one to want one. Did I miss an invasion?"

"No, just the mayor's singles weekend."

He nodded once, tugging at his unruly beard. "I see. Did you participate?"

I spluttered. "What? No."

"Why not?"

Heat flushed my cheeks. "We both know the answer to that."

He cocked an eyebrow. "Ah, so you're finally with Aiden and Finn?"

If he had told me he'd married a duck I couldn't have been more surprised.

"What! No! I mean, what?"

He began to chuckle then abruptly cut off, his mouth dropping open as his eyes widened. "Who is that?"

I glanced behind me to see Colleen navigating her way slowly down the sidewalk.

"Oh, that's Colleen." I turned back to him.

"You should ask Warrick to introduce you since he was sniffing around her earlier today."

"Excuse me." Del brushed past, hurrying after the woman.

I stayed where I was, leaning back against the stone building as I tried to process the barrage of information that had been tossed my way over the last twenty-four hours and which had fundamentally shaken my world to its core.

You're finally with Aiden and Finn.

If Del, who had zero concept of town gossip, knew about Finn and Aiden's interest then….

"It has to be true."

And that could mean only one thing.

Spinning on the loose gravel, I hurried back to my cottage, my mind whirling.

It was time to claim my men.

I tore through my house, searching drawers and spilling underwear and clothing out across my bed and floor.

I owned precisely two dresses—one I wore to weddings and the other funerals. And neither were fit for the purpose I had in mind.

"Damn."

I pinched the bridge of my nose, hating that on the night I most wanted to be sexy I had zero outfits to wear.

"This is pathetic." I threw some old jeans at the wall and plopped on the end of my bed, groaning as I ran my hands through my hair repeatedly. "They want me as I am. Which means they should be happy to take me as I am every day."

I lifted my head to see my old coveralls hanging off the back of my wardrobe door. They were more than a decade old, and I rarely wore them as they were far too tight to allow me to maneuver freely in the workshop.

They zipped at the front, and I felt confident wearing them—and when I wore a particular set of underwear underneath, surprisingly sexy.

"Fuck it," I muttered, pushing off the bed and reaching for the coveralls. "I can only be me."

Dressed from top to toe in an outfit that made me feel powerful, sexy and confident, I locked up my house and returned to the pub. Pushing through the door, I stood in the middle of the nearly empty room and immediately located the two men I most wanted in the world. They stood conversing behind the bar, cleaning up. Upon seeing me, they both stopped what they were doing and straightened.

Ignoring the few remaining stragglers, I strode across to the bar and slid up on my favorite bar stool, watching as they made their way over to me.

My heart pounded in my chest, my belly a riot of nerves.

"You okay, Ry?" Aiden asked, his gaze sweeping over me. "You disappeared."

"I went home to change," I said, ignoring my breathy tone.

Breathe, Riley. You have this.

"Ah." He flicked his dishcloth over his shoulder and leaned into the bar. "Any particular reason why?"

Summoning all my courage, I leaned in, waiting to speak until Finn moved closer to hear my response.

"To fulfill a fantasy."

Their jaws locked tight, their eyes blazing with heat and promise.

Finn's hands clenched and unclenched where they rested on the bar top, like he's trying to restrain himself. Aiden physically rocked back, crossing his arms over his chest, his tattoos flexing as his biceps pulsed.

I hid a smile at, relaxing slightly at their reaction.

"And that might be?" Finn prompted.

"Watching both of you strip me naked."

They were both silent for a long beat—so long I began to doubt myself. Then Aiden reached under the bar and pulled out the giant bell.

Ringing it twice, he turned to the room at large.

"Everyone out!" he shouted. "We're closed!"

Relief hit me hard, and I became grateful for the bar stool under my butt as my legs turned to jelly.

The remaining patrons lifted their heads, grumbling. Hands moved to wallets, and the stragglers began moving to the bar to close their tabs.

"On the house!" Finn hollered. "Just get the *fuck* out!"

Cheering, the customers left quickly as Aiden and Finn ushered them like two-legged sheep dogs toward the door.

Heat pooled in my abdomen while a pleasurable throbbing beat set my blood alight.

They want me.

I felt almost giddy as the last patron exited the bar.

Finn slammed the heavy lock home while Aiden closed all the curtains and hit the lights, sealing us into our own little world.

I took a deep breath as they slowly stalked toward me, their wordless approach sending shivers of anticipatory desire shimmering down my spine.

"Stay there," Finn ordered as I made a move to slip off my stool. "Aiden, get her boots."

"Yes, sir," Aiden said cheekily, dropping to his knees before me. "Hello, gorgeous," he murmured, glancing up at me as he wrapped one hand around my calf. "Let's get Cinderella out of her slippers."

Finn crowded in behind me, shifting until he left only a breath of space between our bodies. My eyelids drifted to half-mast, finding the heat radiating from him—from both of them— intoxicating.

Finn's hands found the zipper of my coveralls while Aiden worked the laces of my boots, slowly peeling them one by one.

"You have no idea," Finn said, his voice rough with desire, "how many fucking times we've talked about stripping these fucking suits from your body."

With my boots off, Aiden tugged the socks from my feet, then wrapped his strong fingers around my arch, massaging the ball of my foot.

I moaned in pleasure, my head falling back as the glorious sensations his talented fingers coupled with Finn's filthy words to evoke a delicious sensory delight.

"Such a good girl," Finn praised as he slowly unzipped my suit, inch by tantalizing inch. The cool air in the pub rushed against my heated skin, causing goosebumps to rise all over my body.

Finn's hand trailed along my collarbone, dipping down towards my chest, the backs of his hands gliding along my skin.

"Fuck."

I smiled at his curse. "Sorry, did I forget to do something?"

"Naughty fucking girl," he admonished.

I'd forgone underwear—or any sort of clothing at all under the coveralls, deciding that I wanted to surprise them as much as they did me.

Finn's palm slid against my jaw, turning my head until his warm lips captured mine. He mouth took possession with a slow, greedy kiss that tasted of barely retrained control, and delicious seduction.

Whimpering, I tilted my head back, wanting more. Wanting him, wanting Aiden, wanting these two men more than I'd ever thought possible.

"I'm yours," I mumbled against his lips. "Yours and Aiden's."

I wrapped one arm around Finn's neck and tangled my other hand in Aiden's hair as a low growl escaped Finn. He deepened our kiss, tasting me and claiming me as his own. His hands were rough as he pushed the coveralls down to my hips, his hands coming back up to tease my breasts.

Aiden's hands left my feet and moved slowly up my body until they could fist in the material of my suit.

"Raise her up," Finn told Aiden against my lips without breaking our deep, hungry, delicious kiss.

Aiden diligently worked the material down, stripping me until I sat naked between them.

"Your turn," Finn said, finally pulling back and turning me on the seat to face Aiden. "I'm going to pay some attention to these beautiful breasts."

Aiden caught my lips in a hungry, hard kiss, stealing my breath. While we kissed, Finn moved to my front to kiss my breasts, teasing my nipples and stroking my inflamed skin.

I began to lose track of whose hands were whose, whose lips were on mine, and whose skin I touched and teased as we became intertwined.

Aiden wrapped his arms around my hips, pulling me to the edge of my seat. Gently, he spread my thighs open while Finn's hand slipped between my legs.

"God, you're so fucking wet," Aiden growled against my ear. "You have no idea how long we've wanted this."

I bit his earlobe, unnecessarily pleased when he shuddered, groaning.

"Naughty girl," Finn chastised. His fingers glanced over my rosy-pink areola. "For the record," he leaned in to press a kiss to my erect nipple, "this is my favorite shade of pink."

I gasped as his mouth closed around my breast.

Aiden, never one to be outdone, dipped his finger to my aching clit, tracing slow, tantalizing circles.

Pants and whimpers escaped my lips as I arched, my hips pumping upward in need. "Please," I begged, desperately. "Please fuck me."

"Oh, we'll fuck you, Riley," Aiden promised, stepping away. "But first…"

He dropped to his knees before me as he slid two fingers inside me. I cried out at the delicious intrusion. He leaned in, his tongue joining his fingers to swirl around my clit.

"You taste so damn good," he said between strokes. "Like my fucking fantasy come to life."

"Our fantasy," Finn corrected, lifting his head from my overly sensitive breasts. "Lick her until she comes. I want to taste her pleasure on your tongue."

The visual of them kissing, combined with the eroticism, drove me to the edge. My hands tangled in Finn's hair as I arched into the exquisite pleasure of Aiden's mouth.

Finn captured my mouth in a kiss, swallowing my screams and begging cries as Aiden worked my clit until I came in an earth-shattering mess.

"Such a good girl," Finn praised, his voice thick with lust. "Good fucking girl."

"Going to fuck her so hard, Finn," Aiden growled, my thighs clenching around his head in response to his growled pleasure. "Tight, slippery cunt."

"Come up here and let me taste," Finn ordered.

They shifted, keeping a hand on me as they wrapped each other in a tight, almost violent one-handed embrace. Their mouths met, and I watched Finn lick my cream from Aiden's lips, both of them groaning.

Aiden's knuckles grazed against my knee, while Finn's fingers tangled in my hair, holding me in place to watch them.

This had to be the most erotic moment I'd ever experienced in my life.

They're mine.

The possessive thought began to fill the hole

that loneliness had carved in my chest. These were my men.

Mine.

"Enough," Finn grunted, pulling away from Aiden. "Let's move this upstairs."

He easily picked me up, holding me in his arms as if I were a bride on her wedding night.

Aiden led the way, opening and then locking doors, and turning off lights as we exited the pub through a set of thick, soundproofed doors, and moved through a long corridor to their house.

I'd only ever been inside their home a handful of times, but I loved it. The house reflected the care they'd taken with my own small cottage, each part lovingly restored. But where my small home lacked space, theirs more than made up for it with five bedrooms, three bathrooms, and its own beautiful cottage garden—once again separated from the pub by a high stone wall.

Finn carried me to his—no, their—bedroom, and gently placed me on the bed.

"Now," he murmured, brushing the hair from my face. "Take Aiden's pants off."

A hot spear of need shot straight to my core. I shuffled forward on the bed as Aiden stepped closer, watching me with greedy eyes.

"Take your shirt off," I whispered.

"You wish is my command." He tugged his shirt off to reveal his powerful torso covered in colorful, fanciful tattoos.

"Oh," I sucked in a breath. "These are beautiful."

He caught my hand, kissing my fingers before placing my palm against his chest. "You can choose my next one."

I had no words for how much his offer meant to me. Instead of responding, I dropped my head and reached for his belt, tugging it free.

Licking my lips, I tossed the leather over my shoulder then began to pull his zip down, revealing the hard outline of his cock pressed against his boxer briefs.

"Mm," I murmured, squirming in place. "Is this for me?"

Aiden made to answer but seemed to lose all power of speech as I slipped my fingers into the band of his briefs, pulling them down to free his cock.

And what a cock it was. Thick, heavy, and proud, I gripped the base, ignoring the slide of Aiden's clothing or the shimmer of his hips as he attempted to divest himself of their weight.

"Condom," Finn barked but I shook my head.

"Are you clear?" I asked, glancing between them.

They both nodded.

"Same. And I have an IUD." I wanted them in me without any barriers. "You okay if we forgo the latex?"

"Fuck yes," Aiden growled.

"Lick his tip," Finn ordered, offering his consent from the end of the bed.

I did as directed, touching my tongue against the salty, hot tip of Aiden's cock.

Aiden's hips jerked and he cursed, his hands shifting to fist my hair. Accepting his silent plea, I opened my mouth, groaning when he slid easily in.

"Good girl, Riley," Finn praised. "You look so beautiful choking on his cock. You want to be a naughty girl and suck him off, don't you?"

I whimpered as liquid desire shot through my body and pooled deep in my abdomen. My thighs clenched, and I could feel the slick wet heat on my skin.

I ached for this. I wanted a cock in my mouth and one in my pussy. I wanted two pairs of hands, two mouths, two everything.

I wanted them. Now.

"Suck him," Finn demanded. "Take him as deep as you can get, and you might receive a reward."

Moaning, I swallowed Aiden down.

"How's she feel, Ads?" Finn asked, a slight curl of taunting in his tone.

"Fucking incredible." Aiden pulled back slightly to cup my cheek. "Keep going."

I had no intention of stopping.

"You look gorgeous sucking his dick, Riley," Finn remarked, as he began to circle the bed. "But you'd look even better with mine stretching your tight, needy pussy."

A guttural groan slipped out of my chest while my hips rocked against the bed. I needed both of them in me—now.

Finn's hands glided over my back. "Follow me."

He gently moved me into a doggy position, Aiden at my front, Finn at my back. I tilted my head up to see Aiden fisting his cock, his gaze on Finn. Twisting, I looked behind me, the breath catching in my lungs.

He was beautiful.

No tattoos decorated his skin—but then he needed none because his body was the art. I didn't know what I'd done in a previous life to be granted this boon, but I was taking it—and them —with both hands and hanging on for dear life.

Please let this last.

Finn's hands glided over the curve of my ass and up my back to gather my hair in one fist. Gently, ever so gently, he moved my head until my mouth lined up with Aiden's cock.

"You sure about this, Riley?" he asked, his voice low and easy. "You say no and this all stops. Anytime. Promise."

I rocked back on my knees, gratified when my ass met his thighs.

"I'm an enthusiastic consenter," I said, grinding my ass against his legs. "I need both of you—right now. Or I swear I will burn this house down if I'm not satisfied within the next five minutes."

Chuckling, Finn pulled gently but firmly on my hair.

"Noted." His voice dropped an octave. "Aiden, you heard our woman. Let's please her."

Aiden's hands dropped to my face, cupping each cheek as he guided my mouth back to his cock. As I swallowed him, teasing his crown, Finn did the same to me, running his knuckles through my slick heat until he found my clit and began to tease.

"Oh, baby," he chuckled. "You're so fucking wet for us. Do you need my cock in you, pretty girl? Do you want your mouth full of Aiden while I fuck this pretty pussy?"

I whimpered around the cock in my mouth, my sucking frantic and disjointed. Aiden groaned, chuckling. "You're distracting her, dude. Either put up or shut up—my dick can't take much more of this fucking pleasure."

"Ask nicely," Finn ordered him.

Aiden's cock flexed in my mouth, and I could taste his pleasure on my tongue at Finn's tone. For all he was a switch, it appeared Aiden quite enjoyed Finn's dominance.

"Please fuck Riley."

I spread my thighs and shook my ass, hoping Finn would get my wordless invitation as I doubled my efforts.

"You fucking—"

Together they pushed in, breaching my two holes in one deliciously startling movement.

Finn's cock stretched me, forcing me wide and hitting every delicious nerve ending as he worked himself inside.

Screaming, panting, sucking, I rocked back

and forth on my hands and knees, taking each deeper with every movement.

I wanted them to lose control. I wanted them to fill me, to mark me, to devour me.

I wanted to set them alight and watch as I burnt their world down. After tonight, they'd have no choice but to rebuild their relationship with me in it.

"Fuck," Finn cursed, slipping his hand around my side to cup my pussy. "She's so fucking close, Aiden. Give it to her. I want our girl satisfied—now!"

Aiden followed his orders and they picked up their game, teasing my back, my sides, my breasts. Aiden worked my top while Finn caressed my rear—playing with my clit and dancing fingers across my lower back.

Filthy words of praise spilled from their lips, driving me higher as they built us up, moving harder, faster, deeper…

I shattered, screaming around Aiden's cock as my body bucked and clenched, lost in the rage of pleasure. Cum shot down my throat, and I automatically swallowed. Behind me, Finn gripped my hips, holding me in place as his cock spasmed in my pussy.

I felt like a badass queen knowing these two gorgeous men wanted me.

We collapsed on the bed, limbs tangled.

"Wow," Aiden finally croaked. "I'm pretty sure I strained something."

"I know I did," I murmured against his throat. "But I'm game to try again."

Chuckling, Finn shuffled us until we were all under the covers—Aiden on one side, Finn on the other, and me in the middle of this man-meat sandwich.

He played with my hair while Aiden gently ran fingers down my side, tracing patterns against across my skin.

"You okay?" Finn asked against my ear.

I nodded, lying.

I wasn't. This felt incredible, special, unique—not to mention unreal and terrifying.

Aiden pulled me into him, snuggling close.

"Sleep," he whispered in my ear as Finn rested a hand on my hip. "We've got you."

Rather than feeling claustrophobic or hemmed in, their bodies made me felt safe, protected, cared for.

With a sigh, I closed my tired eyes and drifted off to sleep.

CHAPTER 7

The early morning sunlight filtered through the curtains, casting a warm glow across the tangled sheets. I blinked awake, momentarily disoriented by the unfamiliar surroundings. As the fog of sleep cleared, memories of the previous night came rushing back, bringing with them a flood of conflicting emotions.

I was nestled between Aiden and Finn, their warm bodies bracketing mine. Aiden's arm was draped across my waist, while Finn's breath tickled the back of my neck. The intimacy of our embrace was both comforting and terrifying.

What am I doing?

Carefully, I extricated myself from their embrace, trying not to wake them. I needed space to think, to process the whirlwind of our supposed courtship—not to mention the fact they'd apparently been flirting with me for months—perhaps even years.

Locating my coveralls from where they'd been discarded on the floor, I slipped them on and crept out of the bedroom.

The house was quiet as I made my way to the kitchen. I found the kettle and set about brewing a pot of loose leaf tea, the familiar routine giving me something to focus on besides the tumult in my mind.

What am I doing? This isn't me. What happens if it goes tits up? I'll be left with a broken heart.

The doubts multiplied as I leaned against the counter, waiting for the water to boil.

What if this was just a one-time thing for them? What if they regretted it in the harsh light of day? What if I wasn't enough for both of them? And even if they did want me, how would this work? Could I be with two men? It might be a tradition in our town, but I certainly hadn't been with more than one person at a time.

I wasn't sure how to function in a one-to-one relationship, let around a triad.

The kettle whistled, startling me out of my spiraling thoughts.

I poured myself a mug and moved to sit at the kitchen table, wrapping my hands around the warm ceramic.

"You're thinking too loud."

I jumped at the sound of Finn's voice, nearly spilling my drink. He stood in the doorway, wearing only a pair of sweatpants, his hair adorably mussed from sleep.

"Sorry," I mumbled, dropping my gaze to my mug. "I didn't mean to wake you."

He crossed the room and poured himself a cup, adding a splash of milk before joining me at the table.

"You didn't. I always wake up early. Bakers hours, Aiden calls them." He studied me for a moment. "Want to tell me what's going on in that beautiful head of yours?"

I bit my lip, unsure how to voice the maelstrom of doubts swirling in my mind. "I... I'm not sure where to start."

Finn reached out, gently taking one of my hands in his. "How about at the beginning? What's the first thought that crossed your mind when you woke up this morning?"

I took a deep breath, steeling myself. "Panic," I admitted softly. "I panicked."

His thumb traced soothing circles on the back of my hand. "Why?"

"Because..." I struggled to find the words. "Because this is everything I've ever wanted, and I'm terrified it's not real. That I'll wake up and it will all have been a dream, or that you and Aiden will realize you've made a mistake."

Finn's expression softened. "Oh, Riley. Is that what you think? That we'd regret being with you?"

I shrugged, feeling small and vulnerable. "It's not exactly a conventional situation, is it? And

I'm... well, I'm me. Grease-stained mechanic Riley, who's been one of the guys for so long I'm not sure I know how to be anything else."

"You're right, it's not conventional," Finn agreed. "But that doesn't make it any less real or meaningful. And as for you being 'just one of the guys'..." He shook his head. "Riley, you've never been 'just' anything to us. You're extraordinary."

His words warmed something inside me, but the doubts still lingered.

"But how would this work? I don't want to come between you and Aiden."

"Good morning, beautiful people," Aiden's cheerful voice interrupted us as he sauntered into the kitchen. He dropped a kiss on top of my head before moving to pour himself some tea. "What'd I miss?"

Finn gave my hand a gentle squeeze. "Riley's having doubts about us."

Aiden's eyebrows shot up as he turned to face us. "Doubts? About what?"

I sighed, running a hand through my tangled hair. "About... everything. How this would work, what people would say, whether I'm enough for both of you."

Aiden pulled out a chair and sat down, his expression serious. "Okay, let's tackle this one thing at a time. First off, how this would work is pretty simple – we'd be together, all three of us. Equal partners in this relationship."

"But what about the practical stuff?" I pressed. "Where would we live? How would we handle finances? What about if one of us wants kids someday but the others don't?"

"Those are all valid questions," Finn said calmly. "And they're things we'd figure out together, as a unit. We don't have to have all the answers right now, Riley. We can take it one day at a time."

Aiden nodded in agreement. "Exactly. As for where we'd live, well.' He waved a hand around his head. "This house has plenty of room. Or we could look for a new place together if you'd prefer. Finances, we'd work out a system that's fair to everyone. And kids? That's a conversation for further down the line, but Finn and I stand firmly on the pro-side of the equation."

I glanced at Finn who nodded his agreement. I absorbed their words, feeling some of the tension in my chest ease. But there was still one nagging doubt.

"What about what people will say? You'll have to go off the island at some point—and neither of you are from here. Your families might have something to say about this."

Aiden snorted. "You know I haven't spoken to my parents since the inheritance was announced."

"And mine couldn't give a shit, so long as I'm happy," Finn said, raising his mug to his lips. "You're protesting for the sake of protesting, Ry."

"No, I'm not," I muttered petulantly.

Finn leaned forward. "Look at me."

I met his gaze reluctantly.

"The only people whose opinions matter in this relationship are the three of us. Yes, people might talk. They always do. But we're not doing anything wrong or illegal. We're three consenting adults who care about each other. Anyone who has a problem with that can fuck off."

A startled laugh escaped me. Aiden grinned, reaching out to ruffle my hair. "There's our girl. Look, Ry, we get that this is a big change. It's okay to be scared. Hell, we're a little scared too. But we want this – want you – more than we're afraid of what might go wrong."

"Really?" I asked, hating how small my voice sounded.

"Really," Finn confirmed. "We've wanted this for a long time, Riley. We just didn't think you felt the same way."

I swallowed, still trying to reconcile my desires with my new reality.

"I need some time," I said, uncertain as to why exactly I needed it but wanting it all the same. "I'm not saying no. I want this but...." I tried to find the words.

"It's a lot." Aiden topped up my cup. "You take all the time you need, Ry. We're not going anywhere."

I raised my mug, breathing in the familiar scent of tea. The doubts I had were mine and mine alone—and I needed to battle those demons.

"Oh shit," Aiden said suddenly, jerking upright. "What time is it?"

I glanced at the clock on the wall. "Just past seven, why?"

"Crap," he groaned. "We've got that breakfast thing for the singles in less than an hour."

Reality came crashing back, reminding me of the world beyond this kitchen. "Oh God, the singles weekend. I completely forgot."

Finn chuckled, pressing a kiss to my temple. "Duty calls, I'm afraid. But how about we have dinner tonight, just the three of us? The pub is closed, and we can talk more about... everything."

I nodded, feeling a mix of reluctance and anticipation. "That sounds good."

"Great," Aiden said, already moving towards the door. "I'll grab a quick shower. Finn, you need a hand with food prep?"

Finn shook his head. "I prepped yesterday. It's pastries, fruit, cereals. All we need to do is assemble and warm some of it up."

"Do you need me?"

Finn shook his head again. We should be able to handle it."

I stood, stretching out the kinks in my back. "In which case, I'll head home."

Finn watched me. "You don't want to shower here? I'm sure we could find you something to wear."

The offer was tempting, but I needed a bit of space to clear my head. "Thanks, but I think I'll pass. I've got clean clothes at the cottage."

He nodded. "Alright. We'll see you tonight."

I moved towards the door, then hesitated. Gathering my courage, I turned back and crossed the kitchen to where Finn stood. Rising on my tiptoes, I pressed a soft kiss to his lips.

"Thank you," I murmured. "For everything."

His smile was soft and warm. "Anytime, Riley. Always."

Feeling bold, I poked my head into the bathroom where Aiden was showering. "See you at breakfast, handsome!"

His delighted laugh followed me out of the house.

The morning air was crisp as I made my way back to my cottage. Deciding to take a quick walk around the town rather than go straight home, I wandered down the cobble stone street, listening to the birds and the quiet murmurings of a town just beginning to wake.

My feet led me towards my favorite place— my workshop. Inside those walls, I was in control. I had confidence in who I was, what I could do, who I could be.

I rounded the corner and to my surprise, I saw lights on inside, despite the early hour. Curiosity piqued, I pushed open the door, the familiar smell of oil and metal enveloping me.

"Dad?" I called out, spotting him bent over the engine of old Mr. Johnson's truck.

He straightened, wiping his hands on a rag as he turned to face me. "Riley? What are you doing here?"

Had amazing, mindblowing, incredible sex with

two gorgeous men who want me and now I'm battling imposter syndrome and contemplating running away because the fantasy was great but the reality is scary and overwhelming?

I shrugged, moving further into the shop. "Couldn't sleep. Thought I'd take a walk."

He studied me for a moment, his eyes narrowing slightly. "Everything alright, sweetheart?"

I hesitated, unsure how to answer. Dad and I had always been close, especially after Mom died, but we'd never really talked about relationships or love. It had always felt like a taboo subject, too painful for us to broach.

"I... I don't know," I admitted.

Dad pointed at the bench. "Grab that lamp and come hold it while I work. Damned eyes are getting old."

I did as told, positioning myself to give him the best light.

He bent back over the engine, muttering to himself as he examined the pipes.

"You going to tell me about it?" he asked.

"No. Maybe? No."

He snorted, leaning further into engine bay. "Shit or get off the pot, Ry."

I took a deep breath, steeling myself. "It's about Aiden and Finn."

His head came up, his eyebrows rising. "Oh?"

Heat flooded my cheeks. "We... something happened last night. Between the three of us."

Understanding dawned on his face. "Ah. I see."

We stood in silence for a moment, the only sound the ticking of the old clock on the wall.

"Are you happy?" Dad asked finally.

I examined his face, noting his shock of thinning white hair and the additional wrinkles that time had carved into his face.

For decades it had been just the two of us, now I had a chance to double our family—and I wasn't sure how he'd react.

I nodded slowly. "I think so. But I'm also terrified."

"Of what?"

I swallowed hard against the lump that had formed in my throat. "I know I shouldn't—but the thought of losing them…. I know what I lost when Mum died. But you? It was like your light blinked out."

Dad stiffened beside me, and I immediately regretted my words. "I'm sorry, I didn't mean—"

"No," he interrupted gently. "No, you're right to be scared. Losing your mother… it nearly destroyed me."

I blinked, surprised by his candor. We'd never talked about Mom's death, not like this.

"But you know what?" he continued, his voice soft. "If I had the choice, knowing how it would end, knowing the pain that would come. I'd do it all over again in a heartbeat."

I turned to look at him, seeing the mixture of pain and love in his eyes. "Really?"

He nodded. "Really. The years I had with your mother were the happiest of my life. The pain of losing her was... indescribable. But the joy of loving her? That was worth everything."

I felt a tear slip down my cheek. "I've been so afraid to take a chance," I admitted.

Dad wrapped an arm around my shoulders, pulling me close. "Oh, sweetheart. I'm so sorry. I never meant for my grief to hold you back from finding love."

I leaned into him, letting out a shaky breath. "It's not your fault, Dad. I just... I didn't know how to open myself up." I chuckled dryly. "I'm not exactly known as the warm-fuzzy type."

"You get that from me." He squeezed me tight. "We're echidnas, you and I. Spikey little beasts who just want someone to love what sits under all those prickles."

He was quiet for a moment, his hand rubbing soothing circles on my back.

"Natalie would be so disappointed in me if she knew I'd never taken another chance at love."

I pulled back slightly to look at him. "She would?"

Dad nodded, a wistful smile on his face. "Aye. She always said life was too short not to grab happiness with both hands when you found it. She'd be furious with me for shutting myself away all these years."

I felt a weight I hadn't even realized I'd been

carrying lift from my shoulders. "So... you think I should take a chance? With Aiden and Finn?"

"I think," Dad said slowly, "that if they make you happy, and you care about them, then yes. You should absolutely take that chance." He squeezed my shoulder gently. "Love is precious, Riley. And it's rare to find it once, let alone twice. If you've found two people who love you and who you love in return, don't let fear hold you back."

I took a deep breath, closing my eyes as a calm settle over me.

Don't let fear hold you back.

Opening my eyes, I grinned at him. "Thanks, Dad. I... I needed to hear that."

He pressed a kiss to the top of my head. "Anytime, sweetheart. That's what I'm here for."

We stood in comfortable silence for a few minutes, the familiar sounds and smells of the workshop surrounding us.

"You know," Dad said eventually, a mischievous glint in his eye. "If you're planning on staying I could use some help with this—"

I jumped away, waggling a finger at him. "Not today, old man. It's the weekend. You and I shouldn't be working."

He grumbled something beneath this breath, his lips pulling into a wry smile. "Should I expect that if my daughter is shacking up with the local publican's I might be offered a free glass of ale?"

I chuckled, slowly walking backward towards

the door. "I might be able to sneak you one every now and then."

He waved me off, already turning back to Mr. Johnson's truck. "Go on, get out of here. And Riley?"

I paused at the door, looking back at him.

"I'm proud of you, kiddo. And I know your mother would be too."

With a heart full of love and newfound courage, I stepped out into the morning sunshine, tilting my face toward the sky.

This was my home. And it was time to claim what was mine.

CHAPTER 8

'd jumped the morning ferry to the mainland, and spent the day browsing through the racks of fashion boutiques and lingerie stores, trying to find something worthy of a night of debauchery. Instead, I'd opted for a simple sundress that hugged my curves and emphasized my breasts.

At precisely seven o'clock, I knocked on Aiden and Finn's door. They'd strung gentle twinkling fairy lights across the walk way which was perfumed by the early spring roses which bloomed in the twilight.

The night air had a slight bite to it, reminding me that winter hadn't quite passed. Used to the cool, I'd forgone a cardigan in favor of baring my arms and breasts, fully hoping for an appreciative reaction from my men.

I was 'bringing the capital-D-Drama—as my friend, Rebecca, would say.

Aiden answered, his eyes widening as he took me in.

"Wow," he breathed. "You look incredible."

I stepped inside, a smile playing on my lips.

"Thank you." I flicked his, 'kiss the chef' apron. "You clean up pretty nice yourself."

Finn emerged from the kitchen, wiping his hands on a dish towel. He paused when he saw me, a slow grin spreading across his face. "Hello, Ry."

"Hello, Finn."

They both stared at me appreciatively like hungry wolves, and I felt a blush creep up my neck.

Aiden leaned in, kissing my cheek. I closed my eyes, breathing him in.

"Missed you today," he murmured.

Finn joined us, resting a hand on the small of my back. "We're glad you're here."

They guided me into the candlelit dining room where a beautifully set table awaited, complete with fresh flowers and gleaming place settings. Soft music played in the background, adding to the romantic atmosphere.

"This looks amazing," I said, touched by the effort they had gone to. "You didn't have to go to all this trouble."

"We wanted to," Aiden said, pulling out a chair for me. "This is our official first date after all."

As we settled in and began to eat the delicious

meal they had prepared, conversation flowed easily. Finn and Aiden were like an old married couple, bickering about who contributed to the meal, sharing memories with me about their lives and adventures.

"So who made the first move?" I asked, glancing from one to the other as we sat enjoying the post-meal glow.

"I did," Finn said, leaning back in his chair. He shot Aiden a slow, sexy grin. "Mister Golden Retriever over there was trying to play it cool."

"Says Mister Black Cat," Aiden shot back. "Everytime I tried to flirt with him, the bastard ignored me."

"He tended to flirt during service. And as much as I liked the guy, I liked my fingers a lot more."

Aiden poked his tongue out at Finn. "Spoilsport."

Finn tipped his glass towards him. "You want to tell her what happened?"

I leaned forward, cupping my chin in my hands and bracing my elbows on the table. "Please."

Aiden flushed, and I delighted in his obvious discomfort.

"Ohhh!" I shot a look at Finn. "It must have been naughty."

"It was," he agreed easily, taking a sip of his wine.

"We were working late. He pushed me into

the cooler room and kissed me." Aiden's gaze met Finn's, holding it. "He then drew back and said, 'We can either get this out of our system or turn this into something real. Either way, we need to fuck.'"

My eyebrows rose and I glanced at Finn with new eyes. "Bold of you to assume, sir."

He chuckled. "You weren't the one walking around with a hard on for six months."

I tilted my head to one side. "And yet isn't that what you accused me of giving you last night?"

"No. You've kept us on a hook for the last two years."

I delighted in his grumbled annoyance before turning back to Aiden. "Continue."

He shrugged. "We fucked in the cooler. Then went back to my place." He frowned. "When did you move in?"

Finn lifted one shoulder in a half-shrug. "Does it matter?"

"We decided to give the relationship a real go," Aiden continued. "Took things slow at first, figuring out our dynamic. There were some bumps along the way, but we made it work."

"And then you moved to Kink."

"Mm." Aiden exchanged a fond glance with Finn. "The inheritance was a surprise. But we made it work."

"Though the renovations nearly killed us," Finn muttered. "Never again."

Aiden made a kiss-y face at him. "What's wrong, boo-boo? Don't you love me?"

Finn kissed his middle-finger then flicked him the bird. "Not when you're delaying shit because you can't decide between off white and eggshell white."

I laughed, enjoying their banter. "When did you know you were staying?"

"Truth?" Aiden asked, sobering. "When we met you."

I blinked.

Finn reached across the table to take my hand, his thumb stroking my knuckles. "We're not gonna lie—you through us for a loop, Ry. The first time we brought our car into the shop, we both left thinking, 'Who is this gorgeous grease monkey and how do I get her number?'"

I shook my head. "I had no idea. I thought you were just being friendly.

"Oh, he was friendly alright," Aiden said dryly. "Practically drooling every time you bent over the engine."

Heat flooded my cheeks as Finn shot him a look. "Like you weren't checking out her ass."

Aiden's his eyes twinkling with mischief. "I plead the fifth."

"So you weren't planning on adding someone else to your relationship?" I asked, confused.

"No." Finn kept a hold on my hand. "But we met you and it's like a piece we didn't know we was missing arrived."

They seemed so sure of each other, so

comfortable in their bond that I couldn't imagine them needing me.

"How did you realize you were both on the same page?"

Finn reached over and took Aiden's hand, lacing their fingers together. The simple gesture spoke volumes.

"We discussed it. We're open about what turns us on or who we're attracted to."

"Idras Elba," Aiden admitted. Finn rolled his eyes.

"We communicate our needs and desires, Ry." Finn continued. "It's not a weakness to find someone sexually attractive or want to explore something."

"I'm not open to a relationship where my partners are sleeping with other people," I admitted.

"Neither are we. There's a difference between fantasy and indulging in consensual fun with your partner and crossing a line. We've always been monogamous—and we want to continue to be so, just with you."

My pulse pumped in my ears, my skin suddenly clammy.

This was it. This was the moment where I decided if I was willing to take a chance.

"I want that," I admitted. "I want to be with both of you."

"Thank fuck." Aiden was out of his chair, pulling me up and into him before I could blink.

His mouth met mine in a hungry, greedy, all

consuming kiss. I moaned into his mouth, needing to be close, to be marked, to be branded by these men.

I wanted to be claimed in a way no one can ever mistake.

"We love you, Riley." Finn nuzzled against my shoulder, pressing a gentle kiss to the seam of my neck. "We're not letting you go, baby."

He caught my ass in his hands, boosting me up until I could wrap my legs around Aiden's waist. Gently, he guided us down the hall toward the bedroom.

Aiden dropped us both on the bed, covering my body with his as he continued to make love to my mouth while his hands dancing skillfully across my body.

I lost track of time as we made out until finally I pulled back, pressing a hand to his chest to create space. I shifted until I could sit on my knees in the middle of the bed looking at my men. With a happy sigh, I placed one palm on each of their chests knowing the next words I'd say would be the ones I'd remember when we were old and grey.

"I love you. I've wanted you since the moment I met you. There's nothing I want more than this." I licked my lips. "If I had my way, I'd marry you both tomorrow."

"Sounds good," Aiden said, glancing over at Finn. "You in?"

Finn grinned. "Works for me."

Laughing, they pulled me down, rolling me

between them. Their hands roamed my body, leaving trails of fire in their wake. Aiden's lips found mine, his kiss deep and passionate, while Finn's mouth traced a sensual path down my neck.

I arched into their touch, my body aflame with desire. Aiden's hand cupped my breast through the thin fabric of my sundress, his thumb teasing my nipple to a hard peak. I gasped into his mouth, overwhelmed by the dual sensations of his touch and Finn's lips on my skin.

"You're so beautiful," Finn murmured against my collarbone, his breath hot against my skin. His hands found the zipper of my dress. "May I?"

I nodded, breathless with anticipation. Together, they slowly peeled the dress from my body, their eyes darkening with lust as they took in the sight of me in nothing but my lacy underwear.

"God, Riley," Aiden breathed, his voice husky with desire. "You're perfect."

Finn hummed in agreement, his fingers tracing the curve of my hip. "Absolutely stunning."

I reached for them, tugging at their clothes.

"Your turn," I said, my voice husky with need. "I want to see you."

They didn't need to be told twice. Shirts were discarded, pants were shed, and soon we were all in various states of undress.

Laughing, I drank in the sight of them –

Aiden's toned body covered in intricate tattoos, Finn's broader frame marked with scars that told stories of a life lived fully.

Finn's hand slid up my thigh, his touch feather-light and teasing. "What do you want, *oeh'uru pahlke*?" he asked, his blue eyes intense as they met mine.

"Everything," I breathed. "I want everything."

Aiden grinned, pressing a kiss to my shoulder. "Then everything you shall have."

They worked in tandem, their touches complementing each other perfectly. Aiden's mouth found my breast, his tongue swirling around my nipple as Finn's fingers danced between my thighs, teasing me through the lace of my underwear.

I writhed between them, lost in a haze of pleasure. My hands explored their bodies, tracing muscles, cataloging scars, my mouth trading kisses and tasting skin. Together we learned what made each of us gasp and moan.

Finn's fingers finally slipped beneath the fabric of my underwear, finding me slick and ready.

"So wet for us," he murmured approvingly, his fingers circling my clit with expert precision.

I cried out, my hips bucking against his hand. Aiden caught my cry with his mouth, kissing me deeply as Finn worked me higher and higher.

"That's it, baby," Aiden encouraged, his voice

rough with desire. "Let go for us. We've got you."

With a keening cry, I shattered, my body convulsing with pleasure as they held me through my release. As I came down from my high, I found them both watching me.

"You're incredible," Finn said, pressing a soft kiss to my lips.

"And we're just getting started," Aiden added with a wicked grin.

"Your turn," I said, nodding at them. "I want to watch you."

Finn's eyes darkened, a slow, predatory smile spreading across his face. "Is that so?" He turned to Aiden, his voice dropping an octave. "On your knees, Ads."

Aiden's eyes sparkled with mischief. "Yes, sir," he quipped, but there was no mistaking the eager way he complied, sinking to his knees before Finn.

I propped myself up on my elbows, my body still thrumming with aftershocks as I watched them. Finn's hand slid into Aiden's hair, gripping it firmly as he guided Aiden's mouth to his cock.

"Show Riley how good you can be for me," Finn commanded, his voice low and authoritative.

Aiden winked at me before taking Finn into his mouth, eliciting a deep groan from the other man. I watched, mesmerized, as Aiden worked Finn's length, his cheeks hollowing with each suck.

Finn's free hand caressed Aiden's face, his touch surprisingly gentle despite his commanding presence. "That's it," he murmured. "Just like that."

I found myself entranced by the interplay between them - Finn's quiet dominance and Aiden's playful submission. It was clear they knew each other's bodies intimately, each touch and movement perfectly choreographed to bring maximum pleasure.

"Touch yourself," Finn ordered, his eyes never leaving Aiden's face.

Aiden pulled back just long enough to quip, "Thought you'd never ask." He leaned forward, pulling Finn back into his mouth and wrapping a hand around his own cock.

The room filled with their gasps and moans, the wet sounds of Aiden's mouth on Finn's cock. I couldn't tear my eyes away from the sight of them together.

"God, you're beautiful together," I murmured, unable to keep silent any longer. My hand snaked down the length of my body to touch the wet heat between my thighs. Whimpering, I drew their gazes, relishing the dark, hungry looks on their faces.

Finn's eyes met mine.

"Come here," he ordered, holding out his hand to me.

I moved closer, and he pulled me up for a searing kiss. I could feel the tension in his body, the way he was holding back as Aiden continued to pleasure him.

"Watch him," Finn murmured against my lips. "Watch how well he takes me."

I looked down at Aiden, who met my gaze with a wink.

Finn's hand tightened in Aiden's hair. "I'm close," he growled. "Swallow it all, Ads."

Aiden hummed in acknowledgment, the vibrations causing Finn to buck his hips. With a guttural moan, Finn came, his body going taut as he spilled down Aiden's throat.

As Finn came down from his high, Aiden sat back on his heels, a self-satisfied grin on his face.

"How was that, boss?" he asked cheekily.

Finn chuckled, pulling Aiden to his feet and into a deep kiss. "Perfect, as always," he murmured against Aiden's lips. "But I believe it's your turn."

Without warning, Finn's hand wrapped around Aiden's cock. Aiden gasped, his hips jerking involuntarily into Finn's firm grip.

"Fuck," he breathed, his head falling back as Finn began to stroke him with practiced ease.

"Eyes on Riley," Finn commanded, his voice low and authoritative. "I want her to see how beautiful you are when you come."

Aiden's gaze locked with mine, his eyes dark with lust and a hint of that ever-present mischief.

"Yes, sir," he managed to say, a small smirk playing at the corners of his mouth despite his obvious pleasure. "Anything you say—" he groaned when Finn gave a particularly ruthless jerk, his head falling back to the bed. "Fuck."

I watched, mesmerized, as Finn worked Aiden's cock. His movements were sure and confident, twisting his wrist on the upstroke in a way that had Aiden panting and moaning. He handled Aiden with care—but his grip was far harder and rougher than any I'd have dared to use.

"That's it," Finn murmured, his free hand sliding around to grip Aiden's ass. "Let go for us, Ads. Show Riley how good you can be."

Aiden's breath came in short, sharp gasps, his body trembling with the effort of holding back. "Finn, I'm gonna—"

"Come for us," Finn ordered, spitting on his hand before he increased the speed of his strokes. "Show us."

With a loud cry, Aiden came, his release spilling over Finn's hand and onto his own stomach. His eyes never left mine as he rode out his orgasm, allowing me to see every flicker of pleasure cross his face.

As Aiden came down from his high, Finn gentled his touch, placing soft kisses along Aiden's neck and shoulder.

"Beautiful," he murmured, before turning to me with a heated gaze. "Don't you think so, Riley?"

I nodded, my throat dry with renewed arousal. "

They both turned to me then, their eyes dark with renewed desire.

"Now," Finn said, his voice husky. "I believe it's time we gave our girl some more attention. What do you say, Ads?"

Aiden's grin was wicked, despite his recent release. "I say we make her scream."

They drew me back down to the bed, their hands and mouths already starting to roam my body.

This was everything I'd ever wanted, and more than I'd ever dared to dream.

"I love you," I said, my voice thick with emotion. "Both of you. So much."

Their answering declarations buried into my heart, searing onto my soul. As they plied my body with playful kisses that turned into sighs, which in turn became moans, I couldn't help but say a little whisper of thanks to the mayor and her crazy plan, and to the fae who'd granted me my deepest wish.

Turns out miracles do happen.

EPILOGUE

The gentle lapping of waves against the shore provided a soothing backdrop as I stood before the full-length mirror, smoothing down the front of my dress. The ivory silk flowed over my curves, I couldn't help but smile as I smoothed a hand over it.

"You look absolutely radiant," my dad said from the doorway, his eyes misty with unshed tears.

I turned to face him, my own eyes welling up. "Don't you dare make me cry, old man. Rebecca will kill me if I ruin my makeup."

Dad chuckled, crossing the room to pull me into a gentle hug. "She wouldn't dare. Not on your wedding day."

As if summoned by her name, there was a soft knock on the door. "Everything okay in there?" Rebecca called.

"We're fine."

'Well, I have someone who isn't. He wants in."

I exchanged an amused glance with Dad. "Let me guess, Aiden?"

"Nope," Finn called. "Try again."

I snorted.

The doorknob wiggled. "Let me in."

"No! No peeking!" I laughed. "It's bad luck!"

"If there's two grooms in this part does that cancel out the bad luck or double it?" Aiden asked from the other side of the door."

I rolled my eyes. "Nice try, boys. You'll see me when everyone else does."

Their grumbling was audible even through the closed door, making me giggle. Dad shook his head, a fond smile on his face.

"Those two really are something else."

"They're perfect," I said softly. "Are you happy, Dad?"

He pulled me into his arms, holding me tight. "Of course, Ry. I'm proud of you, baby. And you couldn't have chosen better—those boys are the kind of men I've always wanted for you." He pulled back just enough to meet my gaze. "Your mother would be so happy for you, sweetheart."

I blinked back tears, pulling him in for another hug. "Thank you, Dad. For everything."

A commotion outside broke the moment, and I heard the mayor's voice rise above the others. "Alright, you two. Back to your places. It's almost time!"

Dad offered me his arm. "Ready to get married?"

I took a deep breath, smoothing down my dress one last time. "More than ready."

The beach was a vision of beauty as we stepped out of the small cottage. Rows of chairs had been set up on the sand, decorated with flowing white fabric and bouquets of wildflowers. An arch made of driftwood stood at the end of the aisle, twined with more flowers and twinkling fairy lights.

As the music began to play - a soft, melodic tune that spoke of love and new beginnings - I saw Aiden and Finn take their places under the arch. My breath caught in my throat at the sight of them.

Aiden looked dashing in a light grey suit, his dark hair tousled by the sea breeze, while Finn stood tall and proud beside him in a matching suit, his blue eyes trained on me.

They were love personified.

Dad squeezed my arm gently, and we began our walk down the aisle. Friends and family from both on and off the island filled the seats, their faces beaming with joy and support.

I saw Mrs. Murdock dabbing at her eyes with a handkerchief, while her husbands each had an arm around her shoulders.

As we reached the arch, Dad placed my hand in Finn's, then took Aiden's as well, joining the three of us together. "Take care of each other," he said, his voice thick with emotion.

"Always," Finn promised.

"We will," Aiden agreed.

The mayor stepped forward, a warm smile on her face as she addressed the gathering. "Friends, family, honored guests. We are gathered here today to witness the union of three souls in the sacred bond of marriage."

She paused, her gaze sweeping over the crowd. "Our island has long recognized that love knows no bounds, that it can encompass more than just two hearts. Today, we celebrate a union that embodies this belief—a triad of love, respect, and commitment."

I felt Aiden's hand squeeze mine gently, while Finn's thumb traced soothing circles on my other palm.

"In our oldest traditions," the mayor continued, "the number three has always held special significance. It represents the phases of life—past, present, and future. The cycles of nature—birth, life, and death. And in a marriage such as this, it symbolizes a union filled with more life, more love, and more strength than any could achieve alone."

She turned to us. "Riley, Aiden, and Finn. You have chosen to forge this bond together, to face life's joys and challenges as one. Do you vow to love, honor, and cherish each other, in sickness and in health, for as long as you all shall live?"

"We do," we said together, our voices strong and sure.

"Then please, share your personal vows with each other."

Aiden went first, his green eyes sparkling with a mix of mischief and deep emotion. "Riley, Finn. I never thought I'd be lucky enough to find one perfect partner, let alone two. You balance me, challenge me, and make me want to be a better man every single day. I vow to always be your rock, your safe harbor, and your partner in crime. I promise to always make you laugh, even on the darkest days, and to love you both with every fiber of my being."

Finn spoke next, his usual calm demeanor softened by the love in his eyes. "Aiden, Riley. You two crashed into my life like a hurricane, turning everything upside down in the best possible way. Aiden, you bring light and laughter to our lives. Riley, you bring strength and passion, setting the example for how to live. Together, you make me whole in a way I never knew I could be. I vow to always be your strength, your comfort, and your biggest supporter. I promise to lead our family with love and understanding, and to cherish every moment we have together."

Finally, it was my turn. I took a deep breath, looking at the two incredible men before me.

"Finn and Aiden. I spent so long feeling like I didn't quite fit, like there was a piece of me missing. Then I found you, and suddenly everything made sense. You complement each other, and together, you complete me. I vow to always be your partner, your lover, and your friend. I promise to face every challenge by your side, to celebrate every victory as if it were my own, and to love you both more fiercely with each passing day."

There wasn't a dry eye on the beach as we finished our vows. The mayor stepped forward again, her voice ringing out clear and strong.

"By the power vested in me by the Royal House, I now pronounce you *o'ech heomei*. You may seal your union with a kiss."

Your forever home.

The ancient phrase seared our souls, binding us together. We were each other's home. Forever.

Aiden pulled me in first, his lips meeting mine in a kiss that was equal parts sweet and passionate. Then Finn's hand cupped my cheek, turning me towards him for a kiss that left me breathless. Finally, they kissed each other, a tender moment that ended with Aiden attempting to playfully lick Finn's cheek. I laughed with the crowd, my heart swelling with love.

As we turned to face our cheering friends and family, the mayor raised her hands for silence. "I present to you, for the first time, Mr. and Mr. and Mrs. Bronze-Sullivan-O'Connor!"

The reception was a joyous affair held under a large tent on the beach. Tables groaned under the weight of local delicacies, while the bar flowed freely with the island's famous spirits.

As the sun began to set, casting a warm

golden glow over the proceedings, Aiden clinked his glass for attention.

"Friends, family, lovely people who are just here for the free booze," he began, eliciting laughter from the crowd. "On behalf of my husband, wife, and myself, I want to thank you all for celebrating with us today."

He paused, his gaze softening as he looked at Finn and me. "I can honestly say I've never been happier or more content."

Finn stood next, wrapping an arm around Aiden's waist. "We've been incredibly blessed, not just in finding each other, but in having such a supportive community around us. Your love means more than we can ever express."

"And speaking of blessings," I said, grinning, "we have one more announcement to make."

A hush fell over the crowd as all eyes turned to us.

"As some of you may have noticed," I continued, "we're expecting a little addition to our family in about five months."

The tent erupted in cheers and congratulations. As the noise died down, someone called out, "who's the father?"

Aiden's eyes twinkled with mischief. "No idea. Shall we take bets?"

There was good natured laughter at his question.

Finn rolled his eyes, though I could see his amusement. "What my delightfully tactless husband means to say is that it doesn't matter.

This child will have three parents who love them unconditionally, regardless of biology."

"Besides," I added, unable to resist joining in on the joke, "we figure we'll know soon enough. If the baby comes out with Aiden's smart mouth or Finn's brooding scowl, we'll have our answer!"

Laughter filled the tent, and I felt a wave of love and contentment wash over me. This was my family - unconventional, perhaps, but perfect in every way that mattered.

As the party continued around us, Finn pulled Aiden and me close.

"Happy?" he murmured, pressing a kiss to my temple.

"Ecstatic," I replied, leaning into his embrace.

Aiden's hand found mine, intertwining our fingers. "Good. Because you're stuck with us now, Mrs. Bronze-O'Connor-Sullivan."

I laughed, squeezing his hand. "Promises, promises."

As the night wore on, we danced and laughed, savoring every moment of our perfect day. And when it came time to cut the cake—a beautiful three-tiered creation decorated with cars, whisks, and beer bottles—we did it together, three hands on the knife, three hearts beating as one.

Later, after the party had died down and the guests had left, we sat together under the stars, sharing a quiet moment on the beach.

"What are you thinking about?" Finn asked softly, his hand warm on the small of my back.

I smiled, looking up at him and then at Aiden. "Just how lucky I am. How lucky we all are."

Aiden pressed a kiss to my cheek. "Luck had nothing to do with it, *oeh'uru pahlke*. We were meant to be."

As I sat there, wrapped in the arms of the two men I loved more than life itself, our child growing strong beneath my heart, I knew he was right. This was always where we were meant to end up—together, bound by love, facing whatever the future might hold as one unbreakable unit.

Three hearts, one love.

And our greatest adventures were yet to come.

I couldn't wait.

Thank you for reading Riley, Finn and Aiden's story!
Want more to know who the baby daddy is?
Check out the bonus on my website
EvieMitchell.com

ABOUT THE AUTHOR

Hey, I'm Evie Mitchell.
I'm a thirty-something romance author
(she/her/hers) living with disability. I believe in
inclusion, accessibility, and fierce romance. My
loves include steamy romance novels, my sexy
husband, our THREE sausage dogs (THE FUR!!!),
and my ever-growing collection of book-related
mugs.

As a woman with a diverse work history,
including in areas such as hospitality, retail,
emergency response, event management, human
rights, disability access, and security—my books
are filled with true stories (bridezillas), worst-
case scenarios (malfunctioning zippers), and my
favorite tropes (one-bed).

I'm a strong proponent of #OwnVoices, and
specialize in fiercely inclusive happily ever afters.

EvieMitchell.com
Socials: @EvieMitchellAuthor

ALSO BY EVIE MITCHELL

All Access Series

Knot My Type

Love Flushed

Darn Knit All

Common Scents

Larsson Siblings

Thunder Thighs

Clean Sweep

The X-List

Reality Check

The Christmas Contract

The A-List

Capricorn Cove

The Shake-up

Double the D

Muffin Top

The Mrs. Clause

New Year, Knew You

Double Breasted

As You Wish

You Sleigh Me

Meat Load

Resolution Revolution

Dogg Pack

Puppy Love

Bad English

The Frock Up

Pier Pressure

Trick or Trent

New Year's Faye

Reigning Hearts

The Marriage Claim

Silent Knight

Men of Trinity Bay

Nameless Souls MC

Runner

Wrath

Ghost

Shield

Elliot Security

Rough Edge

Bleeding Edge

www.ingramcontent.com/pod-product-compliance
Lightning Source LLC
Chambersburg PA
CBHW010438170726
48283CB00011B/3267